Will and Wisdom

what *about* Kindness?

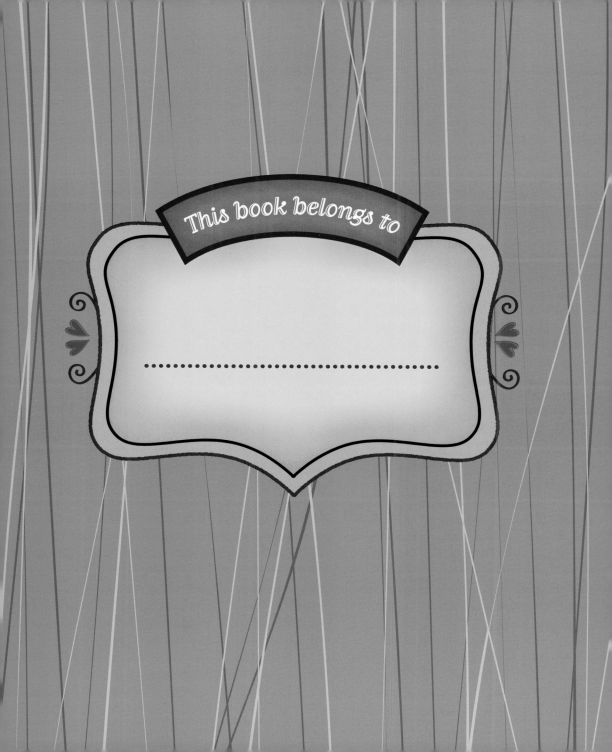

This book belongs to

....

One beautiful fall day, *Will* and

Wisdom were on their way to the park to

play, when they noticed a group of boys

standing in front of Mr. McCurry's house.

Most people in the neighborhood didn't

like Mr. McCurry. They called him,

"Mean Old Mac."

As *Will* and *Wisdom* got closer they could

see Mr. McCurry standing on his front porch

holding a football. "You better give me back my

football, Mean Old Mac," yelled Charlie Kaussen.

"My mom's a lawyer and she will sue you!" The

other boys joined in and were screaming all

sorts of nasty things at Mr. McCurry. "Why don't

you move away!? Nobody in this whole town

likes you!" yelled Johnny Gardner.

☺

Mr. McCurry just stood there looking really sad. Finally, he threw the football to the boys and went inside his house.

The boys mocked him.

"That's right, Mean Old Mac,

you better run inside and hide!"

Charlie yelled. Before they left,

the boys threw rocks and dirt balls

at his house, making a big mess

on the porch.

After the boys left, *Will* put down

his bike and slowly walked toward

Mr. McCurry's house. He grabbed the

broom that was in the corner of the

porch and swept up all of the dirt and

rocks. When he was finished, *Will* put

the broom back and started to leave.

Suddenly, the front door opened and there stood Mr. McCurry. *Will* was a little scared. Mr. McCurry said, "I made you a glass of lemonade." "Oh, thank you," said *Will*. "I'm sorry the guys were mean to you." "I suppose I am partly to blame," said Mr. McCurry. "After all, I haven't been very friendly to them either."

For the next hour, *Will* and Mr. McCurry talked on Mr. McCurry's porch. *Will* found out that Mr. McCurry had played professional football and had been a fighter pilot in the war.

Will also found out that Mr. McCurry

wasn't mean. He was just sad. Five

years ago, his wife had died and now

he was all alone.

Before *Will* left, he asked Mr. McCurry

if he could come back again and talk

about football and flying planes. A big

smile crept across Mr. McCurry's face.

"Bless you son," said Mr. McCurry. "You

are welcome here anytime."

Will walked back to his bike, but before he rode off, he turned and said, "Johnny was wrong." "What do you mean by that?" asked Mr. McCurry. "Johnny said nobody likes you," answered *Will*. "He was wrong, because I like you."

As *Will* rode home, *Wisdom* said,

"Did you know that the Bible says we are

supposed to be kind to everyone?" "Really,"

answered *Will*. "That's nice." "Yes," agreed

Wisdom. "And you are too ."

THE END

Be kind and compassionate
to one another, forgiving each
other, just as in Christ God
forgave you.

Ephesians 4:32

A Prayer To Follow God
and Become a Christian

Dear God,

Help me to be kind and do the right things.
I believe you love me so much that you gave your
only Son, Jesus, to die on the cross for the things
that I have done wrong. Please forgive me and
come into my life and change me. I believe that
Jesus rose from the dead and is coming back some
day. Until then, I will follow you for the rest of my
life. Jesus is my God, my Savior and my forever
Friend. In Jesus' Name, Amen.

_____   _____
your name   date

If you have just prayed that prayer and meant it with all your heart, you are a child of God and will live with Him forever in heaven.

Here's what you can do now:

1. Read the Bible to learn more about God.

2. Go to church and worship with other believers.

3. Be baptized so that others know of your commitment to follow God.

4. Pray everyday and thank the Lord for all that you have.

5. Know that you can do and accomplish anything with God in your life.